Arrive

New York Times & USA Today Bestselling Author

NINA LANE

SNOW QUEEN

PUBLISHING

ISBN: 978-1-7349747-9-9

CHAPTER 1

OLIVIA

"*P*rofessor Hottie alert."

Allie's call rises up the stairs of the Wonderland Café. I leave a pile of birthday party bags on one of the tables in the Wicked Witch's Castle room and peer out the window.

My husband is standing across the street, his tall figure a welcome and familiar sight after a long day at work. Just as I start to ease back from the window, he looks up. Our eyes meet with a spark that kindled into life six years ago and still flares sunshine-bright.

Dean lifts a hand in greeting. I wave at him and head downstairs. Allie is in the reception area, fluffing out her curly red hair with one hand as she pulls open the front door with the other.

"He looks like he's ready for a night out," she remarks, nodding to where Dean is crossing the street. "I hope he's taking you somewhere special."

"Very special." I shrug into my coat. "We're going to a child-birth education class."

Allie gives a little sigh of happiness. "How romantic."

I smile at her before turning to the door. My heart does a little twirl as Dean climbs the front porch steps. Having just come from the university, he's wearing a navy suit and striped tie that somehow has remained unwrinkled despite the fact that it's past six in the evening.

With his thick, brown hair burnished by the streetlights, the masculine planes of his face etched with dusky shadows, he looks both gorgeous and somewhat dangerously sexy. Then he smiles, and his dark eyes crinkle at the corners, and he's my Dean again, all heat and tenderness.

"Hey, beauty." He brushes his lips across my cheek and slides one hand down to my round belly. "All set?"

"All set."

He lifts his head to glance at Allie. "Hey, Allie. How's it going?"

"Just fine, thanks." As usual, Allie blushes a little when Dean talks to her.

"Just let me get my things." I squeeze his arm and head to the front counter, where I'd left my satchel.

When I return, Dean is speaking to Allie in a low tone, which —as his voice usually does—has her gazing at him raptly. She says something in response, then glances up at my approach and gives me a bright smile.

"You guys have a great evening, okay?" she says, waving us toward the door. "Remember if it's a girl, the name Allison would be a perfect fit."

"And we'll change our last name to Wonderland," Dean promises.

Allie grins, and we say our goodbyes before heading outside.

If it's a girl. We don't know if we're having a boy or a girl yet. At Dean's suggestion, we decided to wait until opening night to find out, though that has made my nursery-decorating ideas and baby-stuff purchases varying shades of green and yellow.

He takes my satchel as we walk to his car parked halfway down the block. Black-clad witches, grinning jack-o-lanterns, and spooky ghosts cover the windows of the shops lining Avalon Street.

October in Mirror Lake is crisp and clear as glass, the trees ablaze with red and gold leaves, the downtown streets bustling with activity. Though the Wonderland Café has built up a steady clientele since our June grand opening, business picked up even more when families returned to town after summer vacations.

After we get into the car, Dean drives to the health office on the campus of King's University. I'm well into my sixth month, and everything has progressed smoothly on the baby front.

My girth has increased, of course, I need to pee a lot, and I had to buy a few new pairs of shoes since my old ones no longer fit. My back hurts, and I have to sleep with four pillows to be comfortable. But the baby is fine, my bloodwork is fine, and there is no reason for me to be worried about anything.

Except, you know, giving birth.

I'm not a fan of the weekly childbirth classes, even if there are free cookies and milk. The instructor, Mary, is a lovely, soft-spoken nurse who has been with Labor and Delivery for over twenty-five years. The woman knows what she's talking about.

But what she's talking about are things like dilation and pain management and mucus plugs and the baby *descending* into the birth canal. Like it's going to come out as gently as a balloon losing helium.

Truth be told, I really don't know much about labor and delivery yet. Prior to getting pregnant, I didn't have a reason to learn about it, and the past six months have been so busy with the café and figuring out what to do with our newly purchased (and badly in need of renovation) Butterfly House that I haven't exactly had time to peruse all the pregnancy books I've checked out from the library.

Somewhat guiltily, I glance over the info sheet Mary gave us for tonight's lecture. There are seven other couples in the class with us, all parents-to-be for the first time. We arrange our chairs in a semi-circle around Mary as she takes out a plastic model of the pelvis and shows us how the baby, in this case an infant doll, makes its way into the world.

"Dilation and effacement of the cervix happen together for most women," Mary says. "As we discussed last week, dilation is the opening of the cervix. Who remembers what effacement is?"

Everyone raises their hand except me.

"Dean?" Mary looks at Dean expectantly.

"Thinning of the cervix," he says. "Which is measured in percentages rather than centimeters."

"Correct." Mary beams at him.

Two classes in, and already Professor West is her star student.

"The cervix must soften in order to dilate," she continues, "and often contractions help the process along. Now let's discuss what happens when the mother begins to experience contractions."

I glance at Dean. He's taking notes. Seriously. The man brought a yellow legal pad to class and has already taken two pages of notes. I nudge him with my elbow.

"There's no final exam at the end of this," I whisper.

He looks at me over the tops of his reading glasses. "You're kidding, right?"

"What? There *is* an exam? Mary didn't say anything about that. Is it multiple choice? True or false? Is it an *essay* test?"

"Liv." Dean takes off his glasses. "*Birth* is the final exam."

I stare at him. *Birth* is the final exam.

"Oh." I sit back. "Right."

He's the one taking notes, but I'm the one who actually has to push the little bugger out. And really, if I think about my vagina, and what has been inside it, and the indisputable fact that Dean's erection is a very tight fit…and a baby's head is the size of *a baby's head*…

My heart starts to beat in a nervous rhythm.

I must look a little panicked because he reaches over to squeeze my knee. He's supposed to be all concerned and loving, but instead amusement lights his eyes.

"You can do this," he whispers. "We can do this."

"We?" I hiss. "When your cervix starts dilating and effacing, you can talk about *we*."

"Do you have a question, Liv?" Mary asks from the front of the room, where she is standing with a diagram of a uterus.

"Um, no. No, I'm good. Thanks."

I frown at Dean for getting me in trouble. He winks and returns to his note-taking.

When the class takes a fifteen-minute break, I head for the bathroom with most of the other women. After taking care of business, I dig into the chocolate-chip cookies and milk. Gwen and Marshall, a young couple expecting a girl about a month after my due date, are standing near the table.

"What kind of labor are you planning, Liv?" Gwen asks.

One that results in a healthy baby.

"Just, you know…the usual," I reply.

"We're considering a home water birth," Marshall says.

"A what?"

"It's when the mother sits in a bath of warm water to give birth," Gwen says. "It's a very peaceful, calm way of bringing a baby into the world and it's supposed to ease the pain of labor. I want to keep things as natural as possible. No drugs or anything stressful."

Seems to me drugs would keep things from becoming stressful, but I have a feeling that's not what she wants to hear.

"Well, that's very…thoughtful," I finally say.

"I've done a lot of research," Gwen replies. "I've heard it also helps the baby's transition since water resembles the intrauterine environment. You're due quite a bit sooner than me. Have you done your birth plan yet?"

Guilt nudges at me. I haven't even bought a "birth plan" notebook yet.

Before I can respond, Mary calls the class back to attention and launches into a discussion about early labor symptoms.

"We need to write a birth plan," I tell Dean on the way home.

"I put together a template last week."

"You have a birth plan template? Where do we even start?"

I should know this by now. The fact that I don't makes me feel like I should stay after school for detention.

"We just need to write a list of preferences you want for things like pain management, induction, monitoring," Dean explains. "We'll bring it to the hospital so the nurses know what your choices are." He turns into our garage and parks the car. "You can fill it out when you start making decisions. We'll print out a few copies to put in your suitcase."

I am acutely aware that he's far more prepared for the whole birthing process than I am. Though I cut myself some slack over the fact that I've been busy opening a business and *growing a baby*, I guess there's something to be said for taking notes.

That evening, I do a ton of research on home water births (no, thanks) and birth plans. Following all the links brings up a host of other questions: What's a doula? Do I want one? Hypno-birthing? Walking epidural? Induction options? Do I plan to nurse? How long after giving birth can a woman have sex? How long after giving birth will she *want* to have sex?.

Finally I write up a list of my questions and bring it with me to my check-up with Dr. Nolan the following day. I suspect Dean already knows all the answers, but I'm not about to give him the satisfaction of showing off his knowledge.

After Dr. Nolan patiently answers all my questions, I feel

much more empowered—or at least, ready for next week's class. I go into our apartment, dropping my satchel on the front table.

"How'd it go?" Dean calls through the open door of his office.

"Everything's fine." I stop in the doorway and pat my round belly. "Heartbeat normal, glucose test fine. I've gained twenty pounds, and Dr. Nolan said I should put on one to two pounds a week from now on."

"Might as well do what the good doctor says." He looks meaningfully at my breasts, which have grown bigger right along with the rest of me.

"Lecher."

"Uh huh. Did you tell Dr. Nolan that you're having hot dreams?"

"I most certainly did not." I huff a little at the thought, even though it's true that my dreams have been more erotic than usual lately. "For your information, it's perfectly natural for a woman's libido to increase during pregnancy."

"Oh, I know. Very lucky for me."

Despite the brewing heat in his expression, which under normal circumstances would light my fire good and hot, I mumble something about needing to start dinner before I head into the kitchen. My body has changed more dramatically in the second trimester than it did in the first, and I'm increasingly—sometimes uncomfortably—aware of that fact.

With a sigh, I get a few things prepped for dinner, then go into the bedroom to change into stretch-pants and a more comfortable shirt. As I pull my sweater over my head, I catch a glimpse of myself in the full-length mirror. I'm wearing a sensible cotton support bra, which is pretty much what I wore pre-pregnancy, except this one is larger and my breasts swell over the top of the cups.

Everything else is larger too. I peel off my jeans and stand in front of the mirror in my underwear. The curve of my belly starts beneath my breasts, so it's shaped more like a small watermelon standing on end rather than a beach ball. A few veins show through my skin.

I twist around to look at my behind. Wider and rounder too. Can't say I'm thrilled about that, especially since my ass wasn't exactly flat to begin with. My hips are wider too, not to mention my thighs…

I reach back to unhook my bra and toss it aside. A reddish line from the elastic mars the skin around my back. Soon I'll need bigger maternity bras.

I stare at my naked breasts in the mirror. They're big and pale, also with a few thin veins mapping my skin. Even my nipples are bigger. Darker too.

"You have no idea how sexy you are."

I jump at the sound of Dean's voice and turn. He's standing there with his shoulder against the doorjamb, his arms crossed, and a decidedly heated expression.

"Sexy and fat," I say with a hint of disgruntlement.

"Sexy and *round*," he corrects.

"Round is not sexy."

"Sure it is. Doughnuts are round. And what's sexier than a doughnut?"

I scowl. "I am not a doughnut."

"You're sugary and sweet like a doughnut. Not to mention, you have a delicious hole."

"Dean!"

He grins. "Come here."

"No." I grab for my discarded bra but he gets to me before I can slip it back on.

Next thing I know he's palming my breasts and tugging lightly at my nipples, and then any thoughts of resistance fade into pleasure.

"You are very…" Dean slides his hand over the swell of my belly to my cotton panties. "Very…" his fingers dip below the elastic and apparently he likes what he finds because he groans, "...sexy."

"I think you have a pregnant woman fetish."

"The only thing I have is an Olivia West fetish." He smiles, his eyes darkening with both heat and tenderness.

I get all soft inside like I always do when he smiles at me. But even though his fingers are still doing lovely things between my legs, I wrap my hand around his wrist.

"You don't want to?" He stops his exploration.

"It's not that." Hesitating, I shrug my bathrobe on and fasten the belt. I've always been able to tell him anything, but this is weird, not to mention somewhat unexplored territory.

"What then?" Dean asks.

"I just feel sort of...uh, large."

"Yeah." He takes my hand and presses it against his crotch, which is bulging with an already impressive erection. "Me too."

"Dean, I'm serious. Have you seen the size of my ass lately?"

"Seen it, squeezed it, love it."

"Really?"

"Uh huh." He looks at me and pushes a lock of hair away from my shoulder. "What, you think you don't turn me on just because you're getting bigger?"

"I still have over three months to go. It could get...awkward."

"So we'll figure it out." He pulls me to him and works the knot of my bathrobe, then pushes it off my shoulders. "And if you ever again doubt how sexy you are, all you have to do is get naked. The sight of you makes me hard in half a second."

He slides his hand down into my panties again and teases my folds until my breathing starts to increase. Then he nods toward the mirror.

"Look."

I blush. "Dean..."

"Come on, beauty. You're with me."

It's a reassuring statement, one he's said to me before. One that reminds me Dean is the only person I've ever not only been entirely comfortable with, but often downright uninhibited. Even *raw*.

I glance at the mirror. My heart kicks up in pace. It is kind of sexy, the reflection of me wearing nothing but my panties standing next to my fully clothed husband. My hair is loose and messy around my shoulders, my breasts are heavy, my nipples big and peaked. Dean's hand smooths over the curves of my belly and hips, the white cotton stretched across my bottom. His hard cock is visible through his trousers, his chest rising and falling beneath his shirt.

"See?" He turns me so I'm facing the mirror and palms my breasts in his big hands. "So fucking sexy."

I shudder. He rubs my belly and tangles his fingers into the elastic of my underpants. His erection presses against me, the heat of his skin rolling off him in waves. Lust bolts through me, and I squirm.

"Dean…"

I turn in his arms, stretching upward a little to curve my hand around the back of his neck. I draw him to me for one of our warm, easy kisses that makes my heart race wildly. He moves his hands down to rub my ass, urging my lips apart with his tongue.

I slide into the kiss, my blood warming as if I'm easing between cotton sheets hot from the dryer. I fumble with his belt, then let go so he can unbuckle it. The rasp of leather against fabric sends a shiver down my spine.

Within seconds, I have his cock in my hand and I'm pumping it in the way I know he likes. Arousal coils through me, fierce and tight, and Dean guides us both to the bed. Heat burns in his gaze as he slides his hands over my body, the curves of my breasts and swell of my stomach. He lowers his head to kiss my neck and shoulders, the feather-light touch of his lips causing my tight skin to prickle with sensation.

I want to do the same for him, want to feel his warm, taut skin beneath my lips, so I push him onto his back and move to straddle him. I unfasten his shirt buttons and spread my hands across his chest, tracing the gorgeous muscles with my fingertips. I wiggle a little to rub my bottom against his cock.

"Turn around." His voice is low and rough. "Hands and knees."

Trembling, I climb off him and turn, catching sight of us in the mirror. Dean grabs a couple of pillows and positions them beneath my stomach, then kneels behind me. He rubs his hands over my ass and between my thighs, muttering something about my readiness before he pulls my panties over my hips.

"Jesus, Liv." He slides a finger against my sex. "I could fuck you for hours."

A delicious shiver rocks me. I place my hands flat on the bed and widen my stance as best I can with my panties still twisted around my knees.

I swallow hard. Dean's name comes out on a desperate plea. He reaches around with one hand to toy with my nipples and the other to rub my clit. Sensations crash over me—the rasp of his hot breath on my neck, the brush of his hair-roughened thighs against mine, his adept touch.

I can't stop looking at our reflection. Me on my hands and knees, my breasts dangling like ripe fruits, and Dean kneeling behind me, his shirt half open and his big cock sticking straight out...I moan, squeezing my legs together, aching.

"Dean, please."

He gives a muffled laugh and fists his cock, stroking it up and down with that smooth, rhythmic movement I love so much. I thrust backward, urgency coiling in me like an overwound clock. He grips my ass before pushing forward and filling me with one, delicious thrust.

I gasp. He tightens his hand on my bottom and starts to pump. Through a veil of hair that's fallen over my face, I stare at our reflection in the mirror—Dean's taut muscularity behind me, the sway of my breasts and jostle of my body as he thrusts harder and faster…

I close my eyes and sink into it, letting the arousal build by slow degrees. His thrusts are delicious, hard and measured, creating a sensual friction that has me clenching around him. I rub my breasts against the bedcover to ease the ache in my nipples. Because of my panties in a tangle around my knees, I can't widen my stance, and the friction is even tighter, more intense. Our skin grows shiny with sweat and exertion. My heartbeat pounds inside my head.

"Dean, I can't…oh, please…touch me…"

He slides a hand beneath me to find my clit. A few strokes, and I come with a shriek, convulsing around his shaft. He curses, his fingers still working until he's sure my pleasure has ebbed, and then he grabs my ass again and thrusts deep in a drive toward his own release.

Gasping, I watch in the mirror as our bodies work together one final time before he groans and comes inside me, his chest heaving. I collapse, my body limp and my breathing raspy.

"Damn." He lowers himself beside me and reaches out to fondle one of my breasts. "Never again doubt your own sex appeal."

"Fuck me like that regularly and I won't."

"Such language from the pregnant lady?" Amusement flashes behind the satisfaction in his eyes. "Haven't I been fucking you good for the past six years?"

"Yeah, you do all right." I shift to smile at him, then reach out to stroke a hand over his damp, muscled chest. Astonishingly, a new spark of arousal courses through me. "Glad you can still keep up with me, professor."

"I can't keep my hands off you." He drags his gaze down my body. "I've never been able to."

I roll over to curl against him as we catch our breath, but I don't stay long because these days more than ever I have to attend to certain bodily functions. Especially after sex. I kiss his shoulder and ease away to head into the guest bathroom.

The second I close the door, a tight pain spreads across my stomach.

What the—?

I clutch the doorknob. Dean's name stops in my throat.

I close my eyes for a second and breathe. My heart is still beating hard, and a trickle of sweat runs down my temple. The pain lasts for about a minute and begins to subside. I suck in a lungful of air and splay a hand across my belly.

Latent terror crackles through me—the horror of my miscarriage earlier this year, the knife-sharp pain of loss. I don't move until the cramping stops completely. I take a few breaths, then use the bathroom and splash water on my face.

When I come out of the bathroom, Dean has gone into his office. I turn on my laptop and do a quick internet search about pain during sex while pregnant. Several websites say muscle cramping after an orgasm isn't all that unusual, but I'm supposed to contact my doctor if the pain is particularly bad or doesn't ease. I'm somewhat reassured after learning this, especially since the pain is gone, but the shadow remains.

To banish the lingering fear, I go to the closet and pull out a small box of baby clothes I've already bought—identical onesies and hats in shades of both blue and pink. I sink my hands into the cotton layers, soft as clouds. My tension eases, as if thoughts of the baby are like waves washing gently against the sand, smoothing out all the rough patches.

If it's a girl...
If it's a boy...
...we are so blessed.

CHAPTER 2

Olivia

*O*ctober eases into November with a flurry of work at the café and continued preparations for the baby. Fat, colorful turkeys, smiling pilgrims, and shiny pumpkins decorate the windows of the downtown shops.

As the weeks pass, I take note of any aches and pains I experience. There's some discomfort, but nothing alarming—not even when Dean and I indulge in hot interludes, which continue to be fun and innovative even as I get bigger.

Though my libido is still running on high, the missionary position and a few others are no longer comfortable for me. Our new favorite positions are me straddling and riding Dean facing away from him—which he says he *really* loves because he gets to watch my "magnificent, biteable ass" bounce up and down—or me lying on my side with him entering me from behind, or me kneeling on the sofa, again with him pumping into me from behind, my knees spread wide, Dean's hands gripping my hips and maybe occasionally pausing to give me a little, stinging spank as he pulls back and plunges in again and again...oh, God, *again*...

"Come on, Liv."

His deep voice breaks into my little fantasy. I take a breath, trying to quell the surge of arousal as I pull a brush through my hair. No time for a sexy escapade at the moment, unfortunately.

I hadn't been expecting Allie's call—relayed through Dean an hour ago—that she needs me to take over her shift at the café this morning. Now my plans for a relaxing day spent soaking my feet, eating bon-bons, and seducing my husband have gone by the wayside.

"Liv." Dean sounds irritated.

"Sorry." I leave the bathroom and open the dressing table drawer to look for a crimson ribbon. "I can't help moving a little slower these days."

"A little slower?" He looks at the clock from his position by the bedroom door. "Molasses in January is like Niagara Falls compared to you."

"Way to mix a metaphor, professor."

"It was a simile."

"Whatever." I fasten the ribbon around my ponytail and dab some powder on my nose. "Besides, you try lugging around twenty-five extra pounds and see how fast you move."

"I have to get to the library, and Allie said she needs you to be at the café by eleven because she and Brent have that thing they need to get to."

"What thing?"

"The *thing*." Dean waves his hand impatiently. "And eleven o'clock is seven minutes from now."

"Thank you, Father Time." I make sure my wallet, keys, hairbrush, and lipstick are in my satchel. Then I groan. "I need to pee again."

"Liv."

"This is not within my control!" I glare at him and stomp back to the bathroom.

After peeing for at least the third time this morning, I wash my hands and check my reflection again. I'm wearing one of my work outfits of black maternity pants and long-sleeved, V-neck blouse with a wide sash above my belly. I retie the sash into a bow and go into the living room.

Dean is now waiting by the front door. Looking pointedly at his watch.

"Okay, I'm ready," I announce, glancing at his clothes. "Why are you so dressed up for a trip to the library?"

He looks down at his charcoal-colored slacks, navy blue dress shirt, and gray-and-blue striped tie. With his dark hair brushed away from his forehead, he looks distinguished and handsome as the devil, but…really? The library?

"There's a board meeting I agreed to attend," he says, holding out my coat.

"Since when do you sit on the library board?"

"I don't. They want some advice on their medieval manuscript collection."

I push my feet into my slip-on shoes. "What kind of library board meets on a Saturday morning?"

"The university library board. Now come *on.*"

After grumbling that because I took so long, we don't have time to walk to the café, Dean opens the car door for me and waits until I'm settled before he goes around to the driver's side.

We drive the short distance to Emerald Street, and Dean circles the block twice because of the number of cars lining the street. Not surprising considering it's a bright, beautiful morning. There's a brisk chill in the air, but the sky is eggshell blue, and the sidewalks are humming with shoppers and pedestrians.

"You don't have to park," I say when Dean starts to maneuver the car into a tight space beside the curb. "Just drop me off, then go on to your board meeting."

"It's okay. I have time."

"Five minutes ago, you were snarking at me that you have to get to the library, like, *yesterday* and now suddenly you have time?" I ask peevishly. "Did I miss something? Did we drop through a portal in time and space?"

He puts the car into park and gives me a grin that should come with a warning sign considering the way it makes my heart go all aflutter. I try to maintain my scowl, but then he leans across the console to press his mouth against mine, and of course that's the mortal blow to my irritation.

"If there were a time-travel portal," Dean murmurs against my lips, "I'd travel back to the day we met so I could see you for the first time all over again."

I break away from him to laugh. "You are so full of it."

"Full of love for you, beauty." He winks at me and opens the car door.

We head to the café and climb the steps of the front porch. The doors are closed, which is strange since the café opens at seven on Saturdays.

"Allie didn't tell me no one would be here," I say, fishing in my bag for the key. "Did she tell you anything? Where's the rest of the staff?"

I unlock the door and push it open. The lights are off, and there's a strange hush in the reception area.

"What in the…" I drop my bag on a chair and walk toward the front counter.

An instant later, the lights flare on, a loud cheer fills the air, and I almost pee in my pants.

Dean puts a hand on my shoulder to steady me when I step backward and blink in astonishment.

At least twenty-five people fill the café, along with a blur of pink and blue. Voices rise with laughter, and then Kelsey and Allie appear in my line of vision. To complement the blue streak in her hair, Kelsey is wearing a tailored blue suit and silver jewelry. Not to mention a brilliant and self-satisfied smile. Beside her, Allie is almost clapping her hands with excitement.

"Happy baby shower!" Kelsey encloses me in a hug before reaching behind me to high-five Dean. "Nice work, Professor Marvel."

"She didn't suspect a thing," he says.

I turn to Dean, who is also looking rather smug. "You guys planned all this?"

"Kelsey and Allie did," he replies. "My job was to keep my mouth shut about it and deliver you here on time. Which was no easy feat," he adds.

"Five minutes late." Kelsey shrugs. "We'll forgive you."

"A surprise baby shower?" My heartbeat has calmed down a little, but now my chest is filling with a riot of emotions. "I've never heard of that."

"That's why it was a surprise," Allie says, giving me a tight hug. "We wanted to lure you here at the last minute so you wouldn't have any time to get suspicious."

"It worked." Tears sting my eyes as I gaze at the people, my friends, filling the café Allie and I opened together. "You did this all for me?"

"Yeah, but don't get sappy about it." Kelsey presses a glass into my hand. "Sparkling apple cider. Now go on, mingle. People want to see you and wish you well."

I sniffle and try to compose myself. Dean hands me a tissue.

"You knew about this all along?" I ask.

"Yeah. Kelsey and Allie have been planning it for months. Drove me crazy with the catering menu. Should we have tea sandwiches or deviled eggs or salmon mousse? I picked all three."

"What about the café?"

"Brent just put up a sign saying we're closed until two for a private event, along with a pack of free meal coupons to appease any disgruntled customers," Allie explains. "Now, go on, have fun."

I walk into the café. Even with all the Alice in Wonderland and Wizard of Oz décor—the playing card curtains, curvy high-backed chairs, and colorful murals—I can't get over the way they've transformed the rooms.

The tables are arranged with careful precision, each decorated with a blooming lilac centerpiece and place settings of china, silver, and crystal. Huge bunches of helium-filled pink-and-blue balloons float toward the ceiling. Garlands of pink-and-blue paper lanterns crisscross the molding and provide a soft illumination. Two servers in white jackets walk around with silver trays filled with appetizers.

Dean presses his hand against my lower back to urge me forward.

"Don't you need to get to the library?" I ask. "For the board meeting?"

He chuckles. "There's no board meeting."

"No crying, Liv." A familiar female voice makes me look up. "You'll smear your makeup."

I watch in shock as Dean's mother and sister approach. Joanna West looks lovely in a pale peach dress, her hair carefully styled. Beside her, Paige West is elegant as ever in a cream-colored sheath.

"Congratulations, Liv." Joanna touches my arm and brushes her lips close to my cheek, the air around her smelling like flowers. "We're so pleased everything is going well."

Then, as if I couldn't be shocked any more than I already am, Paige hugs me. These are women who once thought I wasn't good enough for Dean. Somehow, without even being born yet, this baby has bridged a gap that I'd once thought was impassable.

"You look great, Liv," Paige says.

"You...you came here from California for my baby shower?" I ask.

"Our flight got in last night," she explains. "Dean picked us up from the airport."

When I thought he was at a chancellor's reception. I glance at him. The man is smiling like he just pulled off the heist of the century.

And I'm about to become a blubbering mass of goo unless I can pull myself together. I squeeze Paige's hands too tight.

"I'm so glad to see you." I take a breath. "I'm so…I can't believe you came all this way for our baby shower. *Thank* you."

I don't think I can even explain to myself how much their presence means. By the looks on their faces, though, I don't have to.

"We wouldn't have missed it," Joanna says. "Richard sends his best wishes. He'd have come along too, but of course he had to work, and he's still not doing much traveling after his heart attack. We'll catch up later, Liv. I'm sure everyone wants to talk to you."

She and Paige ease back into the crowd. I watch them go, then turn to look at Dean. He reaches out to tuck a lock of hair behind my ear.

"My mother called a few weeks ago," he explains. "She said they'd gotten the invitation and wanted to come."

The fact that Joanna was the one who instigated the trip adds another layer to my surprised pleasure.

"I'm really glad they're here," I say.

"So am I."

I'm not sure even Dean can explain all the complexities behind that simple statement. But then, he doesn't have to. We both already know.

We separate and start to socialize. Everyone I know is here—the café staff, my friends from the Historical Society, all the curators and volunteers from the museum, several colleagues from Dean's department, a few of Kelsey's friends, Allie's father, even the librarian from the public library where I volunteered last year.

And my aunt Stella.

She's standing with her husband Henry near the buffet table. I have to drum up some courage to approach her, especially after everything that happened with my mother last spring.

Though Stella was the one who took me in after I left my mother when I was thirteen, she'd never been able to rid herself of the reminder I was Crystal Winter's daughter—or the belief that I might one day end up like her. For years, I'd feared the same thing, which was the reason I'd spent so long hiding in a shell.

Until I looked out one day and saw Dean.

I glance at him. He's talking to Brent on the other side of the room. The sight of my husband eases my brief anxiety, and I approach my aunt.

"Aunt Stella, thank you so much for coming. You too, Henry. I really appreciate it. I had no idea Kelsey and Allie were going to do all this."

"We're glad for you, Liv," Stella says, pursing her lips.

Henry nods. "Congratulations."

He trundles over to the buffet table to grab a plate. I give Stella a quick hug. "Really. Thanks for coming. It means so much that you're here. I'll always be grateful for what you did for me."

"Yeah, well, you were always a good kid." She squints at me. "You get in touch with your mother?"

I nod, unsure how much I should divulge. But the truth is the truth, so I tell Stella about Crystal's visit and that it ended with a goodbye.

"I don't think I'll ever see her again." I expect the words to hurt, even brace myself for the pain.

But there is none. There's sadness. Maybe pity for the woman my mother has chosen to be. And there's relief that I no longer have to contend with her.

Stella sighs. "Ah well, Liv. That's probably the best kind of relationship you can have with Crystal. No relationship at all."

I stare at her for a moment. Stella hasn't told me much about her own relationship with her sister-in-law—what there was of it, anyway—but I suddenly have the sense it might not have been very different from my own.

"There's only ever been one person Crystal cares about," Stella continues, "and that's Crystal. Took your father a long time to figure that out."

I don't know what to say, so I just nod.

"Anyway," Stella continues. "I hope you'll bring the baby around to visit."

"I will. Of course."

"Good." She heads toward the buffet.

I push thoughts of Crystal away and join several café staff members. I spend the next couple of hours basking in the warmth of friends and family, eating two platefuls of food, and then opening a bunch of presents. There's a lot of laughing and picture-taking followed by cake and coffee.

By the time everyone leaves, I'm starting to yawn. Dean gives my ponytail a gentle tug and kisses the top of my head.

"Ready to go home?" he asks.

I look at the disarray of the hall. "I should help clean up."

"Don't you dare." Kelsey stops by the table with her hands on her hips. "We have cleaners coming in five minutes and, Dean, would you please tell your mother she does *not* have to clear the plates?"

He heads over to where Joanna West is stacking dirty dishes, then gestures to me that he's going to accompany his mother and sister outside. When the cleaners arrive, Kelsey shoos me away so they can get to work.

I give her as tight a hug as my belly will allow.

"I love you." Tears crowd my throat again. "I'm so grateful to have you. Thank you for everything."

"Yeah, well…" Her voice is gruff, but her grip on me is just as tight. "You and that husband of yours are important to me and with a baby on the way, so…whatever. You know."

"Yes." I pull away and smile at her. "I know."

"Go." Kelsey pats my belly and waves me toward the door. "We put the presents in the office, and Dean said he'll come by later to pick them up. I'll call you tomorrow."

I find Allie in the kitchen and give her an equally mushy thank you before I go outside.

Dean is waiting at the bottom of the porch steps for me when I step out into the bright sunshine. For a moment, I just look at him. He's leaning against a post, his hands in his pockets, his tall, lean body relaxed. Sunlight glows on his dark hair. He sees me and smiles.

Even after six years together, the sight of him takes my breath away.

No longer will I harbor any regrets or sorrow about the past. How can I when my past led me to *this* present?

As I walk down the steps, my pulse suddenly stutters. I press a hand to my belly. I've been experiencing this since I was twenty-three weeks pregnant, but every time it happens, it feels like the first time all over again. I stop, curling my hand around the railing.

"Liv?" Dean comes up the porch steps toward me, concern etched on his face.

"I'm okay." I shift my weight and press harder, just below my belly-button on the left side.

A fluttering, like bird wings against my palm. Rhythmic. Soft.

As I always do when Dean is nearby, I take his hand and put it on my belly, then spread my fingers below his as the movement continues—a kicking foot, a waving hand, hiccupping, I don't know what it is, just a gentle, cadenced tapping that reverberates through my arm and directly into my heart.

Hello there, baby. We can't wait to meet you.

CHAPTER 3

OLIVIA

*J*olly Santas, red-nosed reindeers, and smiling snowmen plaster the windows of the shops lining Avalon Street. By early December, a light snow heralds the approach of winter.

With the pregnancy and my business with the café, Dean and I have put our plans to renovate the Butterfly House on hold. The paperwork and process of obtaining permits is both long and daunting, so while Dean still works sometimes on weekends clearing out the house and making plans, we've decided to wait until spring to start the work. Even then, we'll stay in our Avalon Street place for at least the next year.

Thanks to our friends, we have all we need for the baby, and lo and behold everything fits in our little apartment. I put all the newborn clothes in a dresser and packed the others away for when the baby is older. We have a pack-n-play in the bedroom, a swing in the living room, and a bouncy chair by the kitchen table.

Diapers and lotions are arranged on a cart beside the bed, baby books line the bookshelf, and there's a bunch of toys in a box underneath my desk.

I continue to work at the café, though none of my colleagues will let me lift so much as a tea tray. By default, my responsibilities turn more toward office work and payroll while Allie and Brent handle things in the front of the house. I love what Allie and I have created, love the work, my fellow employees, the whole atmosphere of the café.

One afternoon, I head home a little early because I'm accompanying Dean to his department's holiday party. He's already home, so I take a quick shower and dress in black pants and a red maternity blouse with a ruffled neckline.

"Pretty." Dean pats my belly and kisses my temple as I'm fastening on silver earrings. "Pregnancy suits you."

He moves to take his clothes from the closet. I like watching him dress—the adeptness of his fingers as he fastens the buttons, the smooth way he tucks in his shirt and slides his belt through the buckle, the effortlessness with which he knots his silk tie. Then, of course, I like to imagine watching him undress, which is even better.

We drive to a reception room on campus, which the department has reserved for the party. It's a big crowd because collaborating professors and students from other departments have also been invited. There's lots of holiday cheer, sparkling lights, and a great deal of food and eggnog.

Dean gets me a glass of mineral water, then squeezes my hand and heads off to socialize. I make small talk with several people I know, introduce myself to others whom I don't know, and eat a lot of canapés. I glance at Dean from across the room. He catches my gaze and winks. My heart does its usual flip-flop.

I've seen him in this kind of social interaction before, but I forget how good he is at it. He moves from person to person with such ease, his focus intent on whomever he's speaking with, his interest in the subject evident. And people respond to him with admiration, eager to earn his attention, anxious to impress him.

So proud. I am so damn proud of that man.

I turn to introduce myself to a new group of people. For the next few hours, I'm aware of the tide of conversations—often about holiday plans and the like, but also a great deal about medieval studies and research. Musical words float between the clusters of people—*pastoral, mystification, Avignon, allegorical, marginalia, Lindisfarne, Neoplatonic, palimpsest.* It's like they're speaking a secret language.

When the party begins to wind down, Dean finds me again and slides his hand over my lower back. "Ready to go?"

I nod. We say our goodbyes and return home. He pushes the door open for me and tugs at the knot in his necktie as he follows me into the apartment.

"Hey, Dean?"

"Hey, Liv."

"I was thinking...maybe sometime you could tell me about your research."

He pauses in the motion of unbuttoning the top few buttons of his shirt. "I tell you about my research all the time."

"Not *all* the time, you don't." A flush crawls up my neck, and I look past him at the wall. "And, um, when you do I don't always listen."

He doesn't seem surprised to hear this. Maybe my yawning when he talks about Franciscan ideologies is evidence enough of my disinterest.

"So, what, you want to start listening?" he asks.

"Maybe," I reply cautiously. "Working at the historical museum opened up a window for me, you know? I like learning what people did in the past. What they wore, what they ate, how society worked. And I think I'd find your research really interesting if I paid attention to it."

For a minute he just stands there looking at me. An irrational fear rises in me that he might want to keep his work and his home life separate, which of course is stupid since the man works from home much of the time.

"Of course, if you don't want to…" I hasten to add.

"Liv. I'd be happy to talk to you about my research."

"Even if I don't always get it?"

"You don't have to know Latin and Greek to understand medieval history." Dean approaches me and brushes a lock of hair away from my shoulder.

"So maybe we could discuss illuminated manuscripts sometime," I suggest. "When I went to your lecture at the conference, I thought of about ten questions I wanted to ask you."

"So why didn't you?"

"I don't know. They were sort of basic."

A smile tugs at his mouth. "Can I tell you something?"

"Sure."

"I have had two great loves in my life."

"Um." My heart stutters a little. "Two?"

"The first is you," he says. "You're the most important. The one I can't live without."

"Who's the second?"

"Medieval studies." He shrugs. "I know it's not like being a brain surgeon or research scientist. In the grand scheme of things, the relative importance of iconoclastic aesthetics is probably not all that high. But when I went on my first archeological dig and started unearthing objects from hundreds of years ago…it was like I was connecting through time with people who didn't want to be forgotten. Like I had a duty to them."

"And that was it?"

"That was it. Since then, I never once looked back. Never wanted to." He brushes his thumb across my mouth. "Same thing happened with you, Mrs. West."

Oh. I'm melting.

"And I can think of few things I'd like better than to introduce my first love to my second one," he adds.

I smile. "We're sure dorky, aren't we?"

"Uh huh. Good thing we have plenty of explosive sex to counteract that."

A shiver runs through me. Good thing, indeed.

"You know, not that you'll have the time, but you can take a class at King's, if you ever want to," Dean says.

"Any class I want?"

"Any class you want. Just apply as a non-degree student, and you can officially enroll in courses."

"Could I take one of your classes?"

"Sure. Next time I teach I'll be offering my intro class on illuminated manuscripts." He frowns, still rubbing his thumb across my lower lip. "Though don't expect any special treatment."

My lips are starting to tingle. "You mean I won't be the teacher's pet?"

"Oh, you'll be the teacher's pet, all right," he says, "but you'll have to earn your A."

"I've always been a good student."

"I know."

Suddenly it feels like we're no longer talking about illuminated manuscripts.

Though I know I won't have time to really take one of his classes, it's a fun thought. I imagine myself sitting in a lecture hall, my pen poised over my notepad, listening to my husband as he speaks authoritatively about imagery in the *Canterbury Tales*, then strides to the board to write down an arcane word or point out a detail on a slide...

"I'd like that," I murmur, my mouth moving against the pads of his fingers.

"So would I."

He slides his hand across my cheek and around to the back of my neck. Then he pulls me to him for a warm, lovely kiss that makes my heart skip a beat.

His lips brush against mine, back and forth, slow and easy, then he slides his tongue over my lower lip and I open for him. He tastes delicious, like wine and something spicy, and his breath is hot against mine.

I put my hands on his cheeks, rubbing my palms over the faint scratch of whiskers. Warmth travels up my arms. I hold him against me, not wanting to let go, not wanting this blossoming of arousal to fade. Six years together, and the man's kisses make my heart pound as if I've never been kissed before.

He lowers one hand to my belly. The heat of his hand burns through my thin cotton blouse. Already my nipples are straining against the fabric of my bra.

I'm no longer self-conscious of the way I look. How can I be when Dean has never made me feel anything except beautiful and utterly desirable? And, really, I stare at my naked reflection in the mirror at least once a week now…and I do look sexy.

It's weird, maybe, to think of my pregnant body that way but my belly is curved nicely, my legs are well-shaped, my breasts are big and round. My rear end is bigger, but combined with the inward dip of my waist, the extra weight makes my hips flare into curves that fit Dean's hands perfectly.

And my libido still burns hot. *I* still burn hot. For him. I always will.

I move closer to him, inhaling the familiar scent of his shaving soap. I rub my cheek against his, kiss his neck, feel his hands sliding smoothly over all the arches of my body. He trails his finger along my arm and grasps my wrist, then guides my hand to the front of his trousers.

I draw in a gasp. He's not getting hard. He *is* hard, rock solid and straining beneath material.

"Heavens," I breathe, palming all that delicious rigidity. "If I'd known talking about medieval studies got you so hot, I really would have paid more attention."

"Didn't know what you were missing, did you?"

"I'll make up for it."

"I know you will."

He cups his hand beneath my chin and lifts my face for another kiss. A gentle, teasing kiss that's a marked contrast to the urgency I can feel in his groin. He runs his tongue across my teeth, licks the corners of my mouth. I squeeze his erection in response and am rewarded with a muffled groan.

"Bedroom," he whispers against my mouth. "Now."

A few steps later, his lips are locked to mine again and I'm tingling all over. Dean slides his hands underneath my shirt to my bare belly, where the skin is taut and so sensitive these days that the touch of his warm palms floods me with sensation.

I reach between us to tug at his belt, but can't get the leather out of the buckle. I break my lips away from his and look down.

"Take it off."

He backs up a step and slides the belt through the buckle, then drops it to the floor. I watch with a pounding heart as he unzips his trousers and pushes them off along with his boxers, kicking both to the side. His erection springs out from under his loose shirttails, blatant and so tempting that my sex tenses with the urge to have him inside me.

I drag my gaze up to his face. He's working the knot of his necktie, about to pull it off.

"Wait," I say.

He pauses.

"Leave it on." He has no idea how good he looks standing there in his loose tie and dress shirt, the top buttons undone to expose the column of his throat, his cock poking stiff and ready from beneath his shirttails.

A grin twitches the corners of his mouth. "It's the professor thing, isn't it?"

"It always was." I move back into his arms. "Oh, yeah, and the *you* thing."

Our lips meet again, and then he's tugging at my shirt and the waistband of my pants. Since my clothes are all either loose or held up with elastic, they're easy to remove and it's a matter of seconds before I'm standing there in my bra and panties.

I lower my hand again to seek his erection, but he backs me up against the bed and eases me down. He hooks his fingers into my panties and pulls them off, his gaze hot on my inner thighs. I part my legs, moving back into a more comfortable position, tightening in readiness for his delicious penetration.

But no. That's not on the professor's agenda. At least, not yet.

He splays his hands over my belly, then goes down on his knees beside the bed.

"Dean!" The first touch of his mouth rockets through me, pleasure zinging along every nerve. I grab the bedcover and twist beneath him, my pulse throbbing as he spreads me open and strokes my pussy with his tongue.

"Oh, god. So good."

I squeeze my eyes shut, thrusting my hips toward him when he slides a finger into me and sucks on my clit. I come fast and hard, a cry tearing from my throat as he continues his sensual ministrations until I float back to earth.

Dean gets to his feet. His cock looks rigid as steel, and his shirt is starting to stick to his chest. His gaze flickers to mine for an instant, and I know what he wants, and then I want it too because it's so fucking sexy…

I squirm back on the bed and fumble to take off my bra. We have to maneuver to get into the right position, then he kneels beside me. I push my breasts together to create a deep valley. Then I stare down as he presses his cock between them and starts to thrust.

Christ. The sight alone almost makes me come again. The hard knob of his erection appears through the tight vise of my flesh. My body jostles with each thrust. His cock slides in and out, repeatedly engulfed within the warm cavern which is becoming slick from a combination of his arousal and my perspiration.

Above me, his shirt is damp with exertion, clinging to the muscles of his chest. His dark hair flops over his forehead, his jaw tightening with effort and increasing need. I press my breasts together tighter and slip my fingers into the crevice to touch his thrusting cock. When I stroke my thumb over the tip, he groans and pulls away, then grabs my hand and wraps my fingers around his shaft.

Breathing hard, we both stare at the rapid movement of my hand as I rub him to orgasm. His groan deepens before sensation shudders through him and he spills onto my breasts.

I'm hot all over again from this little act, and he knows it because his fingers move between my thighs again and soon I'm pumping hard against his hand and shrieking as vibrations rock through me a second time.

I grab his necktie and pull him to me. His mouth comes down on mine, his tongue sweeping inside, his teeth biting on my lower lip. I tighten my grip on his tie and hold on as the pleasure peaks and begins to ebb.

He fondles one of my breasts, tweaking the nipple before easing down beside me. He's breathing hard. So am I.

Then a sudden cramping clutches my stomach. I gasp. My brain flashes back to the last time this happened, and the internet's reassurances that it's normal, but this pain is worse than before, and my stomach feels like stone.

"What?" Dean pushes up to one elbow. "What's wrong?"

"It's…" I put a hand on my belly. "I don't know. A contraction."

"Not a labor contraction." He spreads his hand over mine. "Pregnant women can sometimes have cramping after an orgasm."

"I read about that, but how do you know?"

"I did some research and talked to Dr. Nolan. It's a post-orgasm contraction of your uterus and abdominal muscles."

"You asked the doctor about my orgasms?"

"Yeah. She also said that for some pregnant women, they're very intense. I told her they're always intense for you, thanks to me."

"Dean!"

He grins. "Kidding. But really, I did research this. It's okay."

Even though he's still all sweaty with his hair disheveled and damp, he is implacably calm. Me? Not so much. Even though this has happened before, it hurts more this time, and it's a little scary.

"Liv, breathe. It'll pass."

"Once again, how do you know?" But obviously he does know because he's looked into this in more depth than I have, and his voice is quiet and steady without the faintest hint of alarm.

"Trust me," he says. "Lie down and wait. If you want, I'll call Dr. Nolan and you can talk to her."

I pull on a bathrobe and lie on my side. If the pain doesn't abate in ten minutes, I will have him call the doctor.

My stomach is hard and tight, and I can feel the slow rolling movements of the baby beneath the cramping muscles. My heart is somewhere in my throat. I have the disquieting realization that real labor pains are likely a great deal worse than this.

Dean climbs off the bed and pulls on his boxers, then heads for the kitchen. In a few minutes, he's back with a cup of tea. By then, the tightness has eased a little and I'm breathing more slowly.

"Thanks." I sit up carefully and take a sip of tea. "This happened once before, but it wasn't as bad. I didn't even know what was going on."

"Because you've been avoiding reading about pregnancy." He settles his hand gently on my nape. "I can't say I blame you. There's some daunting stuff out there."

Of course, that hasn't stopped him from doing extensive research. I'm glad to know that, at least. He wouldn't be so calm if he wasn't certain there's nothing to worry about.

He brushes my damp hair away from my neck and forehead. A crease appears between his eyebrows. "Do you want to talk to the doctor?"

"No, the pain is better."

"But are you okay?"

I nod and drink more tea. Truth be told, I'm still unnerved and not at all sure I want to have another orgasm for the duration of the pregnancy. Which sucks because they really are spectacular. But now that this has happened twice, and the second time was worse, I'll probably be too nervous to even relax enough to have one.

Dean continues stroking my hair. "Maybe we should ease up on sex for a while."

I take another breath and rub my belly. "That wouldn't bother you?"

"Not if it's what you need."

I don't know everything I need, but I do know I can't spend the rest of my pregnancy being afraid. I squeeze his arm. "I'm sorry."

"No need to be sorry." He presses his lips against my forehead. "Hell, with all that extra time, I can tell you everything you ever wanted to know about illuminated manuscripts."

CHAPTER 4

DEAN

*A*s the Christmas holidays roll around, more baby gifts arrive at our front door and are organized in the corner of the living room—blankets, a fancy diaper bag, photo frames, mobiles, children's books, baby toys, and clothes.

Liv spends most of winter break clearing out drawers and shelves to store the baby's things. One of her friends gives us a contraption which apparently doubles as either a playpen or crib, and Liv has already set it up in a corner of the bedroom.

When I come out of my office one afternoon, she's sitting on the floor in front of the bookshelf, arranging the numerous board books and picture books we've been given.

I sit beside her and pick up *Goodnight Moon.* "Would you believe I had this when I was a kid?"

She smiles. "Wow. It's older than the Bible, huh?"

I tweak her nose. "I believe *classic* is the preferred term."

I leaf through some of the other books. Most of them have

rhythmic, musical language. I try to imagine reading the words aloud, holding a baby in one arm and a book in the other.

It's still not an image that comes easily, maybe because none of my feelings about fatherhood are easy. Then again, the best parts of my life have also always been the most challenging. I put my hand on Liv's belly.

"To the side a little." She places her hand over mine. The baby shifts and moves. "It's kind of rolling now more than kicking."

I follow the motions for a few minutes. Awed.

I get to my feet and reach down to help Liv stand. We've been taking regular walks together, as a replacement for the hikes we used to take on weekends. We shrug into our coats and head outside into the unseasonably warm December day.

The light snowfalls we've had so far haven't stuck yet, and the streets are clear of ice. We walk along one of the lakeside paths, where a lone sailboat dots the still-unfrozen water. The sun glints off the bare trees forking upward into the clear blue sky.

Liv and I sit at a picnic table by the lake, tucking our hands into the pockets of our coats. She watches the sailboat. I watch her.

Her long hair, several strands escaping her ponytail, drifts around her face. The extra pregnancy weight has rounded out her features, which combined with her thick-lashed brown eyes makes her look kind of doll-like. I let my gaze travel down her neck to the V of her open coat and the swell of her breasts beneath her ruffled blouse.

My cock twitches.

Damn.

I force my gaze away from her and look out at the water. Even though the no-sex thing was my idea, I don't want her to think it's tough on me. We've had days of self-imposed abstinence before, but always at Liv's insistence.

The summer after we first met, she booked us for a week-long stay at a Maine bed-and-breakfast. We both had visions of long drives in the countryside, sailing, eating fresh lobster, lots of sex.

But when we discovered that the bed-and-breakfast was a rickety Victorian house run by a little old lady, and that we were the only guests, Liv balked at the sex part.

Really.

"This will be your room." Mrs. Beechworth led us up the creaking stairs and opened the door of a second-floor room with a flourish.

She was a tiny woman with sensible black shoes, a floral dress, and graying hair pulled back into a bun. She looked like she belonged in a black-and-white movie playing the part of the town's postmistress.

"This is lovely, thank you." Liv dropped her bag on a chair.

It was a nice room with an iron-framed bed, lace curtains, oak furniture, and a woven rug covering the uneven hardwood floor. Mrs. Beechworth walked around showing us the wardrobe and the adjoining bathroom (the size of a closet), telling us breakfast was served at seven and to be sure and have dinner one night at a restaurant called The Crabby Clam.

After Mrs. Beechworth made her way back down the stairs, Liv bustled around unpacking her bag and opening the windows.

I sat on the edge of the bed and tested the springs. They creaked loudly, like an engine needing to be oiled. Liv turned from the window to look at me.

"We'll make it work," I said, shaking the bed experimentally a few more times.

"Dean, we are not having sex in that bed."

"What, you want to try the window-seat instead?" That sounded promising.

"What if Mrs. Beechworth hears us?" she whispered. She sat beside me and bounced up and down. The springs protested with a screech.

"Liv, the woman must be ninety years old. I'm sure she's had sex sometime in the last century. In fact, I know she has."

"Dean!"

"What, you think it would shock her to hear us?"

"Of course it would," she said. "I swear these walls are paper-thin."

"Nah. Houses like this were built rock-solid. You can't hear anything through these walls."

"Oh, yeah? Listen."

We both fell silent, only to hear Mrs. Beechworth's wavery voice drifting through one of the vents from the kitchen. She was apparently talking on the phone.

Liv pinched my arm. "See?"

"We can be quiet," I said. "At least, I can. You'd have some trouble with that."

She glared at me. I grinned. I loved the sound of her gasping little cries that built into shrieks as her arousal grew. Yeah, so neither of us was much for being quiet during sex. Just one of the reasons it was so awesome.

"So, what, we're not having sex for the rest of the week?" I asked.

"Not if Mrs. Beechworth is in the house," Liv said. "And not if she's not, either. What if she comes back while we're doing it and knocks on the door to tell us tea is served?"

"We'll tell her we'll be down in a minute. Or eighty."

"Dean." She looked stern.

"Aw, come on, beauty. This is supposed to be a romantic vacation, right? What's romance without hot sex?"

"You could try to *woo* me, you know." Liv pushed away from the bed and went to the dresser. She peered at herself in the mirror and brushed her long hair. "Actually this might be good for us, now that I think about it."

"Maybe you shouldn't think about it."

"I'm serious. We can just enjoy each other's company without sex getting in the way."

Now it was my turn to glare. "You think sex *gets in the way*? Of what?"

She turned from the dresser and gave me a very sweet look intended to melt some of my irritation.

"I just mean that it'll be an experiment to see how we do without it, that's all," she said. "We'll have fun and avoid shocking our nice proprietor."

I must have still looked annoyed because she approached and put her hands on my shoulders, then insinuated herself between my thighs. Her breasts were level with my face.

"If you're trying to get my mind off sex, this isn't the way to do it," I remarked, curving my hands around to her round ass.

She dropped a kiss on the top of my head and pulled away. "Let's go find out about the lobster boats. I also want to see if there are any tide pools around. I love tide pools. Mrs. Beechworth has a bunch of brochures in the foyer."

She grabbed her satchel and headed out the door. A minute later, I heard her talking with Mrs. Beechworth in the kitchen. Resigned, I shoved off the bed and followed her downstairs.

With Liv's planning, we did have a great week. We went boating, hiking, kayaking, whale watching, fishing. We ate a ton of seafood, visited local museums and aquariums, drove into the countryside.

We had no sex. A few times I tried to feel Liv up when we were lying in the wobbly old bed, but she gave me a glower cold enough to wither my burgeoning erection.

"Did you know Mrs. Beechworth's bedroom is right below ours?" she hissed.

"I'll be quiet, I promise."

"You are not capable of being quiet during sex."

"What if we go into the bathroom?" Even I wasn't sure we could both fit into the tiny bathroom, let alone get into any kind of good-sex position, but I was more than willing to give it a shot.

Liv shifted around and propped herself onto one elbow to look at me. A shaft of moonlight slanted across the bed and shone on her pretty, dark hair. It said something that even though I was aching to bury myself deep inside her, in that instant I was struck by how much I just *liked* her. I knew by then that I loved her, but over the course of the last ten months, she'd become my best friend. Even if she did issue draconian decrees.

"Dean," she said. "I promise you when we get home I'll get naked before we even unpack and you can have your way with me however you want. Okay?"

Fuck. My erection sprang back to life.

"Uh, yeah. Okay."

She nodded, as if satisfied the issue was resolved, then flopped back over to go to sleep. I sneaked my hand beneath the waistband of my pajama pants and grasped my cock.

"Don't do it." Liv's voice drifted back to me. "I don't want Mrs. Beechworth to be horrified when she changes the sheets."

I groaned and unclenched my fingers from my shaft. "You're a pain in the ass, Olivia."

"Uh huh. Just remember what I said. Your way with me. However you want."

That promise got me through the rest of the week, and by the time we got home, even Liv acknowledged she was ready for some action. True to her word, she dropped her bag on the living room sofa and stripped. We spent the next two hours fucking like rabbits and then ordered out for pizza. Totally worth the wait.

Then again, everything about Liv is always worth the wait.

I glance at her round stomach. She's resting one of her hands on the top curve. She does that a lot these days. I'm not even sure she realizes it.

She glances at me and smiles. Her cheeks are pink with cold. It was the fall after our Maine vacation when I saw her with two toddlers at the zoo and knew—in the span of a heartbeat—that she would be an amazing mother one day. For years, that unbreakable truth has lived right in the center of my soul.

I stand and reach for my wife's hand to help her to her feet. She curls her fingers into mine as we walk back toward the car.

~

By the time the year comes to an end, Liv and I have gone for several weeks without sex. I'd thought it would be easy—really, my wife's well-being and sense of calm are all that matter right now—but frankly the woman turns me on.

She complains a lot now about being warm, and at home she walks around in shorts that show off her legs and T-shirts that can't hide her tits, and then there are all those curves and hollows...I often catch myself staring at her as she walks across the room.

Wishing I could haul her onto my lap and let her ride my cock.

Just the thought makes me hard. I've spent a lot of time imagining all the things I want to do to her. I suspect Liv knows this considering how long it takes me to shower these days, but she hasn't mentioned it...or offered to help.

I haven't asked either. I know where it would lead, and that's not a place she wants to go. Awesome as it is.

I run a lot. First thing in the morning, then again after I hit the gym. I'm doing a few rounds on the heavy bag one afternoon when Kelsey strides up to me in her tank-top and exercise shorts, a towel slung around her neck.

"What's going on?" she asks, nodding to my gloved hands. "Third time this week you've pounded that bag like it's your mortal enemy." She frowns, her eyes narrowing. "Is everything okay?"

"Yeah."

"Liv's okay?"

"Sure." *Jab, cross, hook.* "You've seen her. She's great."

Kelsey folds her arms and stares me down. Even behind her glasses, the woman's gaze is a laser beam slicing me in two.

I hold up my hands and back off before she starts guessing.

"It's nothing," I say. "First-time parent nerves."

"I don't believe you. I'm calling Liv tonight."

"Be prepared to hear about her acid reflux." I figure a long phone conversation between them will give me extra time in the shower. "I'm running home."

I leave my duffle bag in my locker and run a well-worn mountain path that leads to a quiet, residential neighborhood near Avalon Street. I jog a few blocks along one of the back streets, then slow to a walk as I approach our apartment.

Liv is on the living room floor, twisting and turning along with a prenatal yoga video.

"Hey." She bends forward, presenting me with the sight of her gorgeous, round ass, the fabric of her pants stretched tight across it. "How was the gym?"

"Fine. Saw Kelsey. She's calling you tonight."

"Good. I wanted to see if she's available for lunch sometime this week." She rolls into another position and spreads her legs.

I head for the shower.

By the time I emerge, Liv is in the kitchen cooking dinner. I pour a couple fingers of scotch. The burn feels good going down.

She's made spaghetti and meatballs, both of which are excellent. I love that she's not only learned how to cook, but that she takes such pride in it. She's eating less now than she did earlier in the pregnancy, but enjoying the food just as much.

I clean the kitchen after dinner, then go into my office to work on my book while Liv watches a couple of sitcoms. She's on the phone with Kelsey by the time I'm done, and because I'm beat after all that working out, I read for half an hour before falling asleep. I've always slept well, deep and dreamless, and it takes a lot to wake me up.

"Dean?" Liv's voice. "Dean."

"Hmph?"

"You're, ah…you're sort of humping my ass, professor."

I wake with a start. My face is buried in Liv's loose hair. One of my hands is clutching a fistful of her nightgown near her hip. My hard cock is pressed tight against her ass.

Shit.

"Sorry." I let her go and shove back to my side of the bed. My heart is pounding, and I might actually be sweating. What the hell…

Oh, yeah.

The memory flares hot and vivid. My cock is so stiff it hurts. I grasp the base and wince as pressure floods my spine.

Liv takes a minute to disentangle herself from her nest of pillows, then she rolls over to face me. "You okay?"

"No." I swallow. "I mean, yeah. Fine."

"You don't look fine." She presses a cool hand to my forehead. "You're hot."

No wonder.

"Are you—" She pauses. Even in the dim light, I'm sure it's impossible to miss the tent I'm making under the thin sheet. Not to mention I've been grinding against her in my sleep.

"Dean," she repeats, her voice throaty and amused, "did *you* have a sex dream?"

I can't respond because if I do, the images will sear through my brain and I'll come all over the sheets. My fingers tighten reflexively on my cock. If I can manage to get out of bed and into the bathroom…

Liv moves closer. The heat of her skin sinks into me. Her breasts press against my arm. Her nipples are hard.

I can't take much more.

"Liv, if you don't get away from me, I'll…"

She puts a hand on my bare chest and slides it down to my groin, moving my hand out of the way. She smells good, like cherries.

"Liv."

"It's okay." Her cool fingers encircle and squeeze my shaft.

I suck in a breath and close my eyes. So fucking good.

I have no idea what she wants, but when I put a hand on her leg and start to pull her nightgown up, she stops me.

"I don't need it, Dean. Not now. But I'll make you feel good."

"You don't want anything?"

"I want you to tell me about your dream."

I open my eyes to stare at her. She's looking at me, her eyes dark, a wicked smile on her lush mouth.

I swallow hard again. "Uh…"

"I've told you a bunch of mine. What was yours?" She leans closer, giving my lower lip a quick swipe with her tongue. "Was I in it?"

"Yeah."

"Was I a princess?"

"No."

"Lady Guinevere? A milkmaid?" Her grip tightens on my cock as she slides her lips over my jaw and down to my damp chest. "Was I a medieval virgin?"

"You were a librarian."

Her laugh is husky and hot against my skin. "Really? Did we do it on the card catalog?"

"The…circulation desk."

"Tell me." She licks the hollow of my throat, right where my pulse is pounding. Her hand starts moving up and down on my shaft. "I hope the library was closed."

"It was."

"So what were you doing there after hours?"

She's kidding, right?

"I…my dreams aren't as detailed as yours."

"Okay." Her thumb circles the head of my cock. Heat courses through my entire body. "So maybe you didn't hear the closing call. You were deep in the stacks, looking for some dusty medieval tome, and when you emerged you realized the lights were off and no one was around anymore."

I'm mildly tempted to ask her how I could have missed the lights dimming when I was looking for a book, but that detail fades into insignificance as her hand slides down to cup my balls.

"Yeah, that's what happened," I agree.

"Then what? Where was I?"

This I remember. "You were putting some books away on a shelf near the circulation desk. Wearing...ah, damn, that's good...a short black skirt and a white, button-down shirt. No bra."

"Hmm." Her hand slides up my shaft again, her fingernails scratching lightly and causing waves of sensation.

"And when you stretched up to put a book on the top shelf, I saw you weren't wearing any panties either."

"Oh." She leans closer, her breasts pressing against my side. Her thick hair falls over my chest. "Well, wasn't I a shameless little slut?"

"Uh huh. Your skirt hiked right up and exposed the curve of your pretty little ass."

"What...what did you do?"

"Watched you shelve more books. Stared at your ass."

"Did you get aroused?"

"Very."

"Then I turned around and saw you watching me?"

"Um, sure." My brain is so fogged with lust I can't think straight. All I remember from my dream was fucking Liv on the desk, but as long as she keeps working my cock the way she is, I'm willing to embellish the story.

"What did I do?" she asks.

"Told me the library was closed, that it was time for me to go.

I brought you the book I wanted to check out. It was about…uh, ranking of sexual positions in the medieval era."

"What was the ranking?"

"Missionary was most acceptable…standing was considered deviant." I can't help myself from reaching around her to fondle one of her tits. "You told me you'd always wanted to be deviant."

That's about all the embellishing I can manage right now. Liv's hand is working faster, and my shaft is slick and pulsing. Her breath is hot on my neck.

"So what'd you do?" she asks.

"Grabbed hold of your shirt and ripped the buttons off. Your nipples were hard as pebbles, and you pushed your tits into my hands. I fondled and sucked them, then turned you around and bent you over the circulation desk."

This part of the dream is pornographically vivid. I pushed Liv's skirt up to expose her ass, then shoved a knee between her thighs to spread them. She was panting, rubbing her tits on the counter, her pussy open and ready.

"And you fucked me good." She slides her leg over mine.

Yes, I did. I can't get the words out. Sweat drips down my temples. Pressure is building hard and fast. The cherry smell of her fills my head.

Liv moves over to press her mouth against mine. She whispers, "And I was shrieking and writhing as you slammed your hips against me and filled me over and over with your big cock, then pulled out and shot all over my ass… Oh!"

A firestorm explodes in my blood. I come like a fucking torpedo, spilling over her hand and my stomach. Intense waves of heat flood me along with the spasms. I grab the back of her neck and thrust my tongue into her mouth as I pump my cock up into her fist.

"Jesus, Dean." A hard shudder ripples through her body.

I grab her nightgown, certain that she's hot and creaming, but she pulls back and puts her hand on my cheek.

"Don't you want…" I stop.

"Yes, but…not now."

I stare at her. Her skin is flushed, damp strands of hair sticking to her neck, her breathing rapid. I know all I have to do is touch her the right way and…

She eases away from me. Shakes her head.

"I don't think I can."

I take a breath. "I told you it's not…"

"I know. I get it. Really, I do. I'm just being scared. And if you try and I can't, then you'll feel bad."

"I don't feel all that great about not trying."

She smiles. "Believe me, Dean, if I wanted to, I'd have climbed on top of you ten minutes ago. And I know this isn't easy for you, but we've waited this long…I can wait a little while longer." She runs a hand down my chest.

"Yeah, but if you're going to do me like that, you've got to give me something to give back."

"Massages. Foot rubs. Bubble baths. You do the laundry. Let's go have a few nice dinners out. Oh, pick me up those blueberry muffins from Sugar Bakery during your morning runs. I can't get enough of them. Make a playlist of my favorite songs for us to take to the hospital. Maybe arrange for a few restaurants to deliver meals after the baby is born."

"That's it?"

"Oh, I'm sure there's more." She leans in and presses her mouth against mine. "I'll make it worth your while."

"You always do, beauty."

CHAPTER 5

OLIVIA

*I*n January, piles of icy snow line the downtown sidewalks, and the lake has become a skating rink surrounded by white-covered mountains. Hot-chocolate booths sit on the edges of the lake, which resembles a child's spinning toy with all the skaters gliding in circles.

Allie has banned me from the café—a dictate I didn't protest with much fervor since I'm inclined to stick close to home these days.

I'm almost two weeks late. According to Dr. Nolan, I'm one centimeter dilated. She's had me monitored for two non-stress tests, which have indicated the baby is responding fine and the heartbeat is normal. She told me to try some home induction techniques and, if still nothing has happened in a few days, then we'd talk about medical intervention.

I'm anxious. Not really nervous—at least, not as much as I was during childbirth classes—but I'm ready to have this pregnancy over and done with. Dean and I go for a walk around the indoor gym first thing in the morning. I've been exercising regularly throughout the pregnancy, but walking is also supposed to jump-start labor.

The other day Dean brought home two pineapples, claiming he read that there's some enzyme in pineapple that's supposed to "ripen" the cervix.

Dr. Nolan also told us sex can induce labor, as apparently semen helps the cervix ripen, and an orgasm can start contractions. Dean is game to give this a try, but at the moment even the idea of sex exhausts me. I do agree to let him try nipple stimulation—mostly because all I have to do is sit on the sofa with my shirt and bra off.

"The book says to roll the nipples between two fingers." He reaches for his reading glasses, then pages through one of the many books on pregnancy and childbirth we've bought. "Though I read a few things on the internet about different techniques, like stimulating one nipple at a time at certain intervals."

"Dean. I'm sure one technique is as good as another."

"Okay, let's try." He puts the book aside and rubs his forefinger around my nipple. "The book says to pinch and roll them."

"Well, you are a pro at that."

He starts tweaking one of my nipples as if he's turning a radio dial.

Needless to say, I do not find this particularly arousing.

He peers at the open book again, then reaches for my other breast and begins tweaking that nipple too. This continues for about three minutes. I watch him—a crease of concentration between his eyebrows, his dark hair brushing his forehead, his eyes focused behind his glasses.

"Are you getting turned on?" I ask.

"Not at the moment, no."

"Good. Because that would be weird."

"Yes, it would."

Tweak, tweak, tweak.

"Do you feel anything?" he asks.

"Nothing labor related."

Roll, rub, tweak.

"So, uh, this book says you can also try sucking them," he says.

"I most certainly cannot try sucking them."

"I mean, I can suck them." He glances at me. "Or will that freak you out?"

"Not if it doesn't freak you out."

"Actually, it might turn me on."

"Well, that's okay, I guess."

He moves closer to me. We shift around to get into an optimal position before he puts one hand over my left breast and lowers his head to my right. Then he hesitates.

"Dean, you've sucked them before," I say, as if he needs reminding.

"Okay, so…you know, stop me if this gets uncomfortable."

Turns out it's not uncomfortable at all because his mouth is warm and wet, his tongue circling my areola, his teeth biting gently. I don't become a quivering mass of urgency like I usually do when he licks my nipples, nor do I experience even the slightest hint of a contraction, but it's very pleasant and his hair is thick and soft against my chest, his hand resting protectively on my belly.

After a few minutes, he lifts his head. "Anything?"

"No." I glance at his crotch. "You?"

"Uh…"

I can't help smiling. Nice to know I can still get the man aroused, even being over forty weeks pregnant and thirty pounds heavier. Oh, yeah, and almost two bra cup sizes bigger.

Ahem.

I put my hand over Dean's fly, which is starting to swell. I'm still not up for anything acrobatic, but there are certain things I can do that don't require much exertion at all.

His throat works with a swallow. "Liv, you don't have to..."

"I know I don't." But I want to because he's so freaking adorable with his reading glasses on and his hair disheveled and him all concerned about finding the right method of stimulating my nipples.

I squirm around trying to find a good position, but I can't lean over him with my belly in the way. "You might have to..."

"You really want to do this?" he asks.

"Sure. As long as you don't feel like you have to return the favor."

"Well, the book does say that an orgasm will contract your uterus and remember when—"

I stop his words with a kiss. Even though I want to have this baby, I'm still not sure I can relax enough to have an orgasm.

And even though I don't feel like having sex these days, I have never grown tired of kissing my husband. I love the way our lips part at the same time, the way his tongue explores my mouth and his teeth graze my lower lip. I squeeze his crotch, feeling his erection grow beneath the denim of his jeans.

"Stand up," I say.

He does, moving in front of me so I can unbutton his jeans and push them over his hips. My heart speeds up at the sight of his shaft, all warm and rigid. I grasp the base in my hand and lick the tip.

"Ah, fuck, Liv..." Dean spears his hands into my hair and rocks his hips forward. "We were supposed to be stimulating you."

"You, me, what's the difference." I run my tongue over the sinuous veins in the shaft and reach down to cup his heavy balls.

A pulse starts between my legs, but it's mild and more in reaction to his arousal than a direct result of my own.

Maybe.

I curl my fingers into his hips when he starts to gently thrust. It's pretty sexy after all, the sensation of his cock sliding in and out of my mouth, my breasts bare and my nipples decidedly simulated. The pulsing in my sex increases to a throb. A groan rumbles from his chest. I shift to try and rub myself against the sofa cushion.

Dean pauses in his thrusting and looks down at me. "You want more?"

I pull back with a gasp. "I don't know."

"Want me to try?"

I figure it can't hurt. I nod and spread my hands over my breasts. My nipples poke against my palms.

"Should I..."

"Do this." He lifts my breasts and presses them together.

He knows exactly how hot this makes me. My heart starts to pound hard as I feel him slide into the valley between my breasts.

A luscious, warm coil winds through my lower body as he pushes his cock into my cleavage, his hand gripping my hair, his breath coming fast. I love the sight of his erection pushing through the pillowy cushions of my breasts, love the way his fingers dig in tighter when his desire spikes.

He stops and slips away from me. I wiggle backward on the sofa so he can settle beside me, smoothing his hand over my belly down between my legs. I tense a little as he delves his fingers in the pleats of my sex, but his touch is so light and gentle that my anxiety melts away.

"All right?" he whispers.

I nod. He lowers his head to capture my mouth in a deep kiss that makes my blood spark. His tongue sweeps into my mouth. His chest rises and falls against mine, my nipples tingling from the brush of his taut skin. I can feel it, the spiral of arousal beginning to unwind slow and rich, but the shadow of pain lingers.

I put my hand on the side of Dean's neck. His pulse beats hard against my palm. He lifts his head.

"I don't think I—" I start.

"It's okay." He runs his thumb down my cleft, lowers his head to my breasts.

I let my eyes drift closed, even as I know that this desire is going to spin around inside me with nowhere to go, like an endless whirlpool. Even as my body surges, as shivers rain down my spine, I sense the blunt edge of unfulfilled lust.

"Oh, Dean, I'm sorry."

His laugh is hoarse and hot against my breasts. "Ah, sweetie, you have no reason to be sorry."

He pushes his hips against me, and his very stiff erection nudges my thigh. I get the message and grasp his shaft. I squeeze my legs together, longing for the break in tension, the cascade into bliss.

When Dean mutters low against my throat and pumps his cock into my fist, I feel a responding surge deep in the pit of my stomach. One more pull on his shaft, and he comes between us with hard pulses. I love the shuddering of his muscular body, the way he grips my waist, the rough groan vibrating against my skin.

He eases away to catch his breath, his mouth seeking mine as he slips his hand down my abdomen and into my cleft again. Again, his touch is so gentle that my body relaxes.

"Come on, beauty," he whispers, threading his other hand through my hair, his breath warm against my lips. "Let me see you come."

His deep voice settles in my core. With a muffled moan, I spread my legs wider. He slips his forefinger into me. Fresh tension laces through me, that pull toward release that I crave and yet haven't experienced in far too long.

"Oh, Dean." I arch upward, pressing my breasts against him. "I feel it…"

"So fucking beautiful." He lifts his head, his smoldering gaze on mine, his face flushed with heat. "Give it to me, nice and hard."

He increases the pressure, lowering his head and taking my

tight nipple between his teeth. One teasing tug, and a thousand sparks shoot to my core. Before I can stop it, I'm straining toward the crest of bliss.

"Dean, I'm going to come." I grip his shoulders, bucking my hips up into his hand. "Harder, I'm...oh!"

The tension breaks. With a shriek, I come, rapture flooding me in wave after wave of exquisite sensation. Dean's murmurs of pleasure are a steady stream against my breasts as I quake and shudder beneath him. He continues working his fingers between my legs until the wave begins to recede, leaving me panting and sated.

"Oh." I inhale a breath, wiping a trickle of sweat from my temple. "Oh my."

He straightens and slides his hand over my damp belly. His hot gaze drifts over my naked body.

"Well," he remarks, "we might not need the pineapple after all."

CHAPTER 6

OLIVIA

JANUARY 25—3:28 A.M.

"Dean? Dean." I reach across the bed and jostle his shoulder. "Dean!"

"Hmm?" He shifts and rolls toward me, locking his arm around my chest. "Are you having a sex dream? Because I'd be happy to—"

"I'm having a contraction."

"What?" His eyes fly open.

I put a hand on my belly. "It's not strong, but it's definitely a contraction. The orgasm must have worked."

"Really? I know I get you going, but—"

"Dean! It's a *contraction*."

He pushes up to one elbow and puts his hand on my stomach. Then he blinks. "Wait, what the hell am I doing? Where's the stopwatch?"

He grabs the stopwatch from the nightstand drawer. "Hold on. Tell me when the next one starts."

We wait. And wait. When I feel another one start, Dean times it to fifteen seconds. As it turns out, the next one is over half an hour later, so even Professor Neurotic realizes it makes no sense to time each one.

"Not yet, anyway," he says.

Anxiety flutters inside me. I push back the bedcovers. Since I have no idea when we'll need to leave for the hospital, I tell Dean I'm going to take a quick shower.

"Leave the bathroom door open." He also gets out of bed. "Call if you need me. What time is it? Are you hungry? I'll make sure everything's ready for the hospital."

I don't bother reminding him that we've had everything ready for the past three weeks. Clearly the man needs something to do.

I stand under the shower for twenty minutes. The hot water pounding over my hair and skin dilutes some of my nervous tension. I put a hand over my belly when it starts to tighten again.

"Okay, baby," I whisper. "Let's do this."

I get out of the shower and dress in stretchy maternity pants and a T-shirt. A thousands thoughts fly through my brain. How it seems like I've been waiting to meet this baby forever, and yet how quickly the past nine months have gone.

I think about my childhood, remembering faces, names, places, emotions. For the first time in my life, those thoughts aren't accompanied by bitterness or sorrow, but by a kind of complacency. A belonging.

"Five minutes." Dean clicks the stopwatch. He's been showered and dressed for the past two hours. "We should head for the hospital."

It's almost seven in the morning. My contractions hurt but not excessively so, and my water's already broken. After an L&D triage check determines my membranes have ruptured and I'm two centimeters dilated, a nurse named Karen puts me into a birthing room and hooks me up to a fetal monitor. She consults with the doctor, who determines I should be admitted.

"There was a chance I could have been sent home?" I ask Karen.

"Well, sometimes people get a little anxious and come to the hospital too early," she explains, then smiles at Dean. "You did the right thing."

He beams back at her. "I have Liv's birth plan all ready too."

Oh, lord. The man is going to be a legend among Mirror Lake's nurses before long.

He gets the plan out of my suitcase and shows it to Karen. They consult over it for a few minutes before she places it with my medical chart.

"So, uh, what do I do now?" I ask. I've changed into a hospital gown and am sitting propped up against the pillows.

"Relax and keep contracting," Karen says cheerfully. "I'll get all the forms from your file. Anything changed since your pre-admission interview?"

I shake my head.

"How's the pain?"

"Bearable." Of course, I have no idea how long it will stay that way.

"I'll get an IV started, but you'll still be able to move around," Karen says. "Dr. Nolan is delivering twins down the hall. She'll be in as soon as she's available."

After inserting the IV into my arm, she leaves. Dean pulls a chair up beside my bed and sits down. "You need anything?"

"Not yet." I shift around to get comfortable and glance at him. He's staring at me.

"What?" I ask.

"Nothing." He reaches out to push my hair away from my face. "Just…you know."

"Yeah." I squeeze his hand. "I know."

We sit for a while. I tighten my grip on his hand when another contraction clenches hard. The nurse comes in to ask questions, we fill out a few more forms and continue to wait.

After another hour, Dr. Nolan comes in to check on me. She announces that I'm still only three centimeters dilated, even though my first contractions started over five hours ago, and suggests that we do some walking to try and speed things along.

I'm not all that thrilled about walking up and down the hospital corridors, but Dean's already helping me into a pair of slippers before I can protest. He holds my arm and we head out to walk. The hallways are surprisingly quiet—a few doctors and nurses go from room to room, family members returning with cups of coffee, but overall it's calm.

I try and breathe through another contraction. Dean stops. I realize I'm gripping him so hard my fingernails are digging into his arm. He uses his shirtsleeve to wipe sweat off my forehead.

"Want to go back?" he asks.

I suck in air and shake my head. I don't think I'll be able to walk much longer, so I might as well do what I can now. We make a few more laps up and down the hallway, pausing for another contraction, before returning to the room.

I'm not feeling good. I'm sweating, and nausea is starting to roil in the pit of my stomach.

Dr. Nolan comes in for another check. "Still only three centimeters," she says.

The announcement makes me want to cry, especially when another contraction tightens around me like an iron band.

"Can you give her something for the pain?" Dean asks.

"I'll try and get the anesthesiologist in here. Last I checked, he was in surgery." Dr. Nolan glances at the birth plan, then nods. "Sit tight, both of you."

She leaves. I grip my husband's hand, my lifeline, and breathe.

I can't tell if tears or sweat are running down my face. I feel like I'm about to burst out of my own skin. My body is hard as stone, totally foreign. My spine is about to break in two. The hospital gown is sticky and heavy.

I'm vaguely aware of Dean prowling beside my bed. Aware of his hand smoothing my hair back, pressing a wet cloth to my forehead. Aware of the rumble of his voice, deep and soothing against my ear. Aware of the unbreakable grip of his fingers as I seize his hand through the pain. Aware of the fear he's trying to keep contained.

I close my eyes and float on a wave of agony. I can't even swallow. When another contraction yanks a scream from my throat, Dean lets me clutch at him until the pain eases, and then he pulls away and curves my fingers around the bedrail.

"I'm getting the doctor." His tone is rough, but lined with that implacability I know so well. He brushes a kiss against my forehead. "Be right back."

I sink against the pillows and concentrate on breathing. A palpable relief curls through me because I sense some sort of end to this. I know my husband won't let up until he gets someone in here who can ease this horrible pain.

I've lost track of how much time has passed. I hear faint music in the background, but the sound grates against my ears.

Dean's hand touches my hair. "Liv, the anesthesiologist is here."

Oh, thank god.

There's a flurry of activity around me as the anesthesiologist introduces himself, explains the procedure, and instructs me to sit up and hunch over a pillow. Another contraction clutches me. I bury my face in the pillow and breathe through it.

I'm able to answer the anesthesiologist's questions as he preps my back and inserts the needle. The procedure is quick and painless. After the catheter is in place and the medicine given, the nurse and Dean help me lie back down. Already a delicious numbness spreads through me.

"There's another one." Karen consults the monitor after another few minutes. "How do you feel?"

"Okay." There's still a mild pain, but nothing like what it was before. The relief gives me a renewed burst of courage.

"Try and rest now," Karen suggests. "You'll need your strength when it's time to push."

I close my eyes. My chest feels looser, making it easier to breathe, and my body no longer feels like something alien.

"Is that better?" Dean looks at the monitor as he pulls a chair back up beside my bed.

"Yes. God." I push a swath of damp hair away from my forehead. "This is insane."

"Now maybe it'll be a little easier." He looks more stressed out than I've ever seen him before, but when he catches me watching him, he manages a smile. "I'd offer you ice cream, but you're not supposed to eat anything."

"Yeah. That sucks. I think I'm hungry."

I know I'm exhausted. I slip my hand into Dean's, for comfort this time rather than the back-breaking need to get through the pain, and lean against the pillows.

I spend the next few hours dozing, but I'm unable to sink into a deep sleep. The nurse lowers the lights. I sense her and another nurse coming in and out, the machine beeping, the remnants of pain.

Fuzzy images that make no sense cascade through my mind—green apples, a needle and thread, the towers of a cathedral, a spiral staircase, an ant and a grasshopper. I remember that I was supposed to finish the café payroll. I have the irrational thought that we left the coffeepot on. I'm worried that Dean has to get to the university for office hours.

I drag my eyes open. The room is quiet, dim. He's still beside my bed, his dark gaze on my face. He shifts, leans closer.

"Hey," he whispers. "How are you?"

"Will I ever have this baby?"

He strokes my hair. "You will. I promise."

I let my eyes close again. He never tells me something unless he means it. Unless he knows it.

I doze again. When I wake, my mouth is parched, and I have a horrible combination of hunger and nausea. I suck on ice chips and imagine a chocolate milkshake.

Dean sits beside the bed, paces the floor, and only leaves the room to get a cup of coffee. Dr. Nolan stops by intermittently to check on my progress. Twelve hours after I was first admitted, she looks up from another dilation check and smiles.

"Are you ready to have your baby, Liv?"

Dean is at my side in a flash. I tighten my hand on his and nod.

"I'm ready."

CHAPTER 7

OLIVIA

*O*ur son comes into the world after both months and a second. One minute ago, our family was me and Dean, and then—despite the months of pregnancy, the hours of labor that seemed endless, and the final flurry of activity—our boy arrives in what seems like no time at all.

The epidural continues to work its magic as I do everything I'm supposed to do. Even though I obey the nurses' instructions about when to push, when to stop, when to breathe, it feels like part of me is floating above the bed, separate from the mechanics of giving birth but utterly secure in the knowledge that I'm doing everything right.

As always, Dean is a constant, steady presence at my side, his deep voice a stream of love and encouragement in my ear. He leaves me only to check on the progress of things between my legs, and he is as fascinated with that event as he has been with everything else.

My body strains with pressure, work, tension. I sweat, grit my teeth, and push, push, push. Then, when I can hardly inhale another breath, Dr. Nolan looks up at me.

"One more, Liv," she says. "That should do it."

I close my eyes and push. My heart pounds. The pressure releases, a sudden lifting, and then a baby's cry fills the air, my heart, my soul.

I open my eyes. Dr. Nolan holds up a damp, squirming baby boy, the umbilical cord still attaching him to me, and my breath stops in my throat. I stare at the baby, stunned, and then my son opens his eyes and looks right at me with eyes as black as night.

In that instant, I'm both lost and forever found.

I sink back against the pillows. Dr. Nolan hands the baby to one of the nurses, who says something about me needing to breastfeed right away, and there's another bustle of activity and movement before Nicholas is wrapped in a blanket and placed in my arms.

He's both weightless and heavy, like an anchor securing me to the earth. A brilliant, golden streamer of love and hope unfurls, hugging us both in a warm, protective embrace. Not until this moment have I more clearly understood the meaning of the word *wonder*.

"Shift him a little toward you." Karen moves to my side, helping me get Nicholas to latch onto my breast. When he does, his eyes drift closed.

There's a movement at my side. I turn to where Dean is sitting beside the bed, his gaze on Nicholas's face.

For a moment, I stare at my husband. His eyes are red-rimmed and bloodshot, stubble covers his jaw, and his hair is a mess. He has never looked more beautiful.

Dean shifts his gaze to mine.

"Hi," I whisper past the tightness in my throat.

He leans forward and puts a gentle hand on my head, pressing his lips to my forehead.

"I love you so much, Liv." His voice is rough.

"I love you too, Dean."

The words will never be enough to encompass everything we are to each other, but he and I both know all the secret nuances and intricacies that belong to us alone. And the rest of the world fades into the distance.

We look at the baby together. Nicholas's face is pink and scrunched, his eyelashes long and dark against his cheeks, his little hands balled into fists. A sweet, fragrant scent wafts from him. A tuft of dark hair covers his head. As we watch, he starts to squirm. His eyes flutter open to reveal his midnight eyes.

"Hello, Nicholas," I say softly.

He yawns. I glance at Dean with a smile. He's looking at our son as if he's never seen a baby before. His eyes are damp. He shifts his gaze to mine.

And then there just aren't any words at all.

CHAPTER 8

DEAN

*A*fter the nurse takes Nicholas for testing, I leave Liv to rest and go outside for a few minutes. I stand on the sidewalk outside the hospital, breathing the cool evening air and trying to untangle everything I've been feeling for the past day.

My hand shakes as I pull out my cell and scroll my contacts, then press the phone to my ear. "Dad?"

"Dean?" His voice is wary, probably because I never call him when he's still at work. "Is everything okay?"

"Everything is fine," I assure him. "Better than fine. I called to tell you Liv had the baby. A boy."

There's a stunned silence on the other end, as if my father hadn't even known Liv was pregnant. I almost smile.

"Dad?"

He clears his throat. "That's great news. I'm...how did it go?"

"It was rough for Liv, but no complications." I take a breath. "He's six and a half pounds. We named him Nicholas."

"Nicholas West. Good name. Strong."

"Yeah." My throat is starting to close up. "So, uh, I'll give you a call later, okay? I want to tell Mom too."

"Congratulations, son."

I end the call and dial my mother's cell to tell her the news.

"Dean, I'm so happy for you." Her voice thickens with emotion. "I'll let Paige know and tell her you'll call her when things settle down a bit."

"Thanks, Mom."

I hesitate for a second, not sure if I want to make my next request but knowing I'll regret it if I don't. If nothing else, my brother needs to know he has a nephew.

"Hey, you don't happen to have Archer's contact number, do you?" I ask my mother.

"I don't know, dear," she says, her tone edged with worry. "Last time he called me, he was in Texas, I think. Do you want me to try and find out where he's staying?"

"Yeah. I'd like...well, I'd like for him to know about Nicholas."

I don't know what I expect to happen by telling Archer he has a nephew. Maybe nothing. Maybe something. It's been a long time since I've believed anything good might come of my relationship with my brother. I guess having a child does that to a person—gives you a reason to hope.

"I'll do what I can, Dean," my mother says. "Give our best to Liv, and please send pictures. I love you."

"You too, Mom."

I end the call and draw in another few gulps of air. The world still seems out-of-focus, as if it has stopped for the past day and is trying to start again.

I head back to Liv's room. She's asleep, her features pale but relaxed. I stop beside the bed and touch her shoulder.

More emotions than I know what to do with crash through me. Amazement, gratitude, awe, wonder. A love so all-consuming, so fierce, that it has the power to bring me to my knees.

I brush a few strands of hair away from Liv's forehead and graze my fingers against her smooth cheek. A noise sounds from the adjoining room, and I straighten as a nurse enters. She smiles at me.

"He's just in here," she whispers, gesturing behind her.

I follow her into the room, where Nicholas is in his little bassinet. There's a blue knit cap on his head, and he's starting to squirm out of his blanket.

"He'll be hungry by the time Liv wakes up, so we'll bring him in for breastfeeding," the nurse tells me. "You're welcome to have some time with him now. Just press the buzzer if you need anything."

She motions to a buzzer beside a rocking chair and leaves the room. I look at my son for a moment before reaching into the bassinet to pick him up. So small, almost weightless, like a bird nestling into the crook of my arm.

I sit down and rub my hand over the fuzzy tuft of his hair. He blinks up at me. I read somewhere that a baby's eye-color lightens over time. I hope Nicholas's eyes turn a warm, dark brown, just like his mother's.

I examine his fingers and toes, the shell-shape of his ears. I run my finger over his eyebrows and tickle the soles of his feet.

Some part of me is surprised by how natural this feels, how easy. I was so focused on the pregnancy that I haven't allowed myself much time to think about actually holding a baby. But our son fits just right in my arms, he seems to like the movement of the rocking chair, and he's looking at me like he knows exactly who I am.

Like he knows we're going to be the best of friends.

I lower my head. Breathe in his clean baby smell.

"One day I'll teach you how to pitch a baseball," I tell him. "How to knot a necktie. How to kick a field goal. How to tie a lure, ride a bike, and barbeque a steak."

He squirms. I shift him a little and rock in a different rhythm. He yawns.

"I'll try and get you interested in medieval architecture, but it's okay if it bores you," I continue. "I'll explain why the Rolling Stones' *Exile on Main Street* is the best album of all time. I'll build Lego spaceships and tree-houses with you. We'll go on train rides and sailboats. I'll tell you to always do the right thing, but I'll understand when you don't and we'll figure out together how to do better next time."

I brush my lips across his soft hair. "You lucked out with your mother, kid. She's amazing. She's going to do everything right. Me, on the other hand...I'll probably mess up this whole parenting thing sometimes. Sorry in advance for that. But you can also help me figure out how to do better next time. And I promise I will always do the best I can for you. In everything. Okay?"

He yawns again and flexes his tiny hands, then closes one fist tight around my forefinger.

CHAPTER 9

OLIVIA

*P*art of me wants to sit in bed forever with Dean by my side and our baby in my arms, but there's a lot to do and even more to learn. The nurses bring Nicholas in and out for breastfeeding, instructions, tests, bonding. A lactation consultant comes to offer advice about positioning the baby to avoid discomfort, a photographer takes newborn pictures of Nicholas, and delivery people bring flowers and balloons from our friends.

Through it all, Dean sits beside my bed, sometimes holding the baby and sometimes just watching. He doesn't say much, but I can almost see his brain processing everything as Dr. Nolan provides instructions for recovery, and a nurse discusses a very long list of things to be mindful of once we're home with the baby.

Two days pass in much the same way. Dean rarely leaves. He sleeps on a fold-out bed in my room and showers in the adjoining bathroom.

He holds Nicholas whenever he gets a chance, learns how to change a diaper and use a bulb syringe on the baby's stuffy nose. He takes notes about the symptoms that would require a call to the doctor when we're home. He watches carefully whenever I try to nurse, and by the second day he's using terms like "latching on" and "colostrum."

Kelsey comes in with a huge chocolate bar for me and a mild scolding for Dean because he didn't call her right when I went into labor.

"I was a little busy at the time," he remarks dryly.

"You're forgiven. When do I get to meet my godson?"

"I'll ask the nurse to bring him in."

After he leaves, Kelsey brings up a calendar on her phone and shows it to me.

"So I've got a schedule for people to bring you guys dinner," she says. "We're rotating on a four-day basis, and everyone's instructed to bring at least enough for two meals."

"Kelsey, you didn't have to do that."

"Trust me, you'll thank me later." She puts the phone back in her purse. "Allie is trying to get everyone to base their meals around a *theme.* There's enough food in your fridge now for the next five days, but I'll call tomorrow to see if you need anything. And I'm on-call if you want me to take care of the baby while you catch up on sleep or something."

"Thank you so much."

She waves her hand dismissively, as if she knows I'm about to get emotional. The door opens, and a nurse wheels Nicholas's bassinet in. Dean follows.

"Oh my god, he's beautiful." Kelsey reaches into the bassinet to pick up the bundle of baby. After settling him in the crook of her arm, she smells the top of his head and starts cooing at him and making baby noises.

Dean and I exchange amused looks, even though both of us have always known Kelsey is a secret softie.

"Okay, I'm leaving you alone." Kelsey shifts Nicholas carefully back into the bassinet and bends to hug me. "You've got a gorgeous kid there, Liv. Thank the gods he looks like you."

She flashes Dean a smile. He responds with a wink.

"No argument from me," he remarks.

"I'm number one on your contact list, so call if you need me." Kelsey lets Dean give her a bear hug, even responding with one of her own, before she heads off.

Dean brings Nicholas to me, and I get him positioned for another attempt at nursing.

While both Dr. Nolan and the nurses are all lovely and helpful, by the time my discharge time rolls around, I'm very ready to be home. Dean and I pack up our things, and I dress Nicholas in a "newborn" onesie and pants that are so big they hang off his little arms and legs. I settle him in his carry car-seat and buckle the straps.

Among all the many other unexpected things in recent months, I'm surprised by how natural it already is to care for our son—and that had been one of the things I wasn't at all certain I could do.

Turns out there have been a lot of things I wasn't certain I could do—and yet I've discovered I can do them very well indeed.

After I sign the discharge papers, a nurse wheels me to the front door where Dean is waiting with the car. He settles Nicholas in the backseat and opens the passenger side door for me. I shift to get comfortable and pull on my seatbelt.

After Dean closes the door and gets into the driver's seat, he doesn't move. Silence fills the air.

"Dean?" I glance at him.

He's watching me, his dark eyes filled with warmth and tenderness. He holds up his left hand. I put my left hand against his. We twine our fingers together, and our wedding rings make a familiar click that sounds like the bright, gentle ring of a bell.

He brings my hand up and brushes his lips across my fingers, then releases me so he can start the car.

"You, me, and now three, beauty," he says.

"We're a trio." I smile. "Three sides, like a triangle. Isn't a triangle the strongest shape in the universe?"

"According to mathematicians and scientists, maybe," Dean says. "Not according to me."

"So according to Professor West," I ask, "what's the strongest shape in the universe?"

"A heart."

Of course. My beautiful, brilliant husband.

And so we bring our son home, moving together into our new future as parents—a future forever woven with the unbreakable golden thread of Liv and Dean.

ABOUT THE AUTHOR

New York Times & USA Today bestselling author Nina Lane writes hot, sexy romances about professors, bad boys, candy makers, and protective alpha males who find themselves consumed with love for one woman alone. Originally from California, Nina holds a PhD in Art History and an MA in Library and Information Studies, which means she loves both research and organization. She also enjoys traveling and thinks St. Petersburg, Russia is a city everyone should visit at least once. Although Nina would go back to college for another degree because she's that much of a bookworm and a perpetual student, she now lives the happy life of a full-time writer.

www.ninalane.com

facebook.com/ninalaneauthor
twitter.com/ninalaneauthor
instagram.com/ninalaneauthor
amazon.com/author/ninalane
goodreads.com/ninalane

THE SPIRAL OF BLISS SERIES

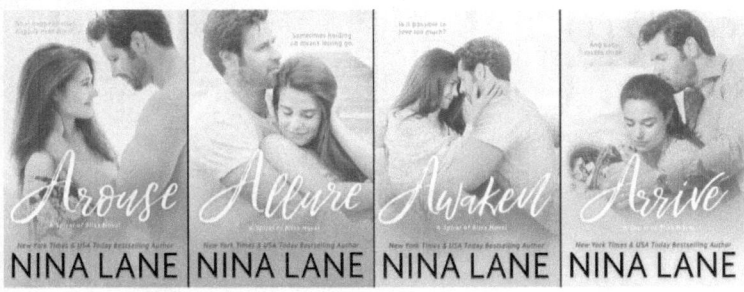

"Give me a kiss, beauty."

From an exhilarating crush to the intensities of marriage, Liv and Dean West embark on a passionate lifelong journey together. As the medieval history professor and his beloved wife face both personal challenges and painful battles, they never lose sight of the hope, humor, and devotion that belong only to them.

Liv and Dean's everlasting romance will melt your heart, turn you on, and enchant you with the power of a love to end all loves.

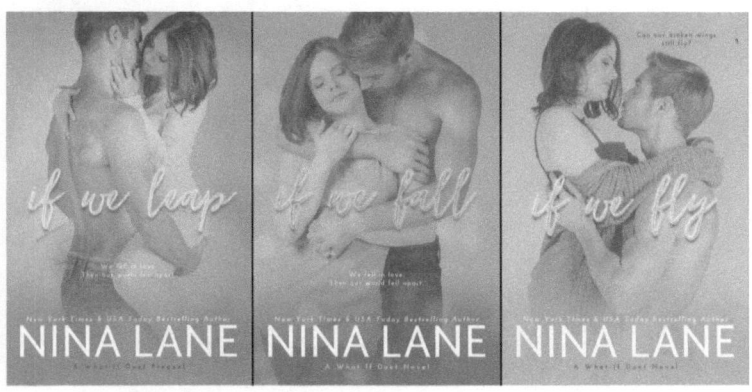

First we fell in love. Then we fell apart.

Shattered by tragedy a decade ago, two lovers fight the secrets that could destroy them.

"This book is a work of art."

A woman fleeing scandal. A town's mysterious recluse.

Lust and secrets collide in this provocative romance.